THIS CANDLEWICK BOOK BELONGS TO

....

For the ARVON FOUNDATION, which
helped make this book happen — J. D. and P. H.

Text copyright © 2018 by Joyce Dunbar
Illustrations copyright © 2018 by Petr Horáček

First U.S. edition 2019

Library of Congress Catalog Card Number pending
ISBN 978-1-5362-0424-7

18 19 20 21 22 23 LEO 10 9 8 7 6 5 4 3 2 1

Printed in Heshan, Guangdong, China

This book was typeset in Sabon and Warugaki.
The illustrations were done in mixed media.

Candlewick Press
99 Dover Street
Somerville, Massachusetts 02144

visit us at www.candlewick.com

CANDLEWICK PRESS

Joyce Dunbar • Petr Horáček

GRUMPY DUCK

Duck was feeling grumpy.
The pond was dry, so she
couldn't paddle in it.
She had no one to play with.

A little gray cloud appeared over her head.

She waddled over to Dog, who was digging a hole.

"I've got no one to play with," she said to Dog.

"You can play with me," said Dog, "if you like digging holes."

"I don't," grumped Duck. "Digging holes would
make my feathers dirty."

"Uh-huh." Dog sighed.

The little gray cloud got **BIGGER.**

Pig was rolling in the mud.

"I've got no one to play with," Duck said to Pig.

"Come and play with me," said Pig, "in my gloopy puddle."

"No, thanks," grumped Duck. "Ducks like water, not gloop."

"Ooooink," honked Pig.

The little gray cloud got even **BIGGER.**

Rooster was cockadoodling.

"I've got no one to play with," said Duck.

"You can play with me if you like," said Rooster.

"We could sing a cockadoodle chorus."

"I just don't do cockadoodling,"
grumped Duck.

"Squawk!" said Rooster.

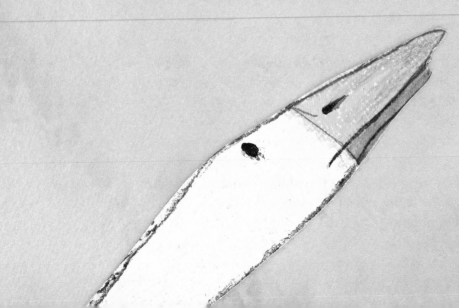

The little gray cloud got **BIGGER** still.

Rabbit was hopping around.

"I've got no one to play with," said Duck.

"Come and hop with me," said Rabbit.

"We can see who can hop the highest."

"*You* can, silly!" grumped Duck.

"I'm *not* silly," said Rabbit.

The little gray cloud
wasn't little
anymore—
it was

BIG.

Tortoise was dozing in his shell.

"I've got no one to play with," said Duck,

tapping his shell with her beak.

"You can doze with me," said Tortoise. "It's very peaceful."

"Boring, more like," grumped Duck.

"Tut," tutted Tortoise.

Now the gray cloud was

HUGE.

"Cheer up, Duck," said Goat, who
was busy eating the washing on the line.
"I've got no one to play with," said Duck.
"Share a snack with me," said Goat.
"Here's a tasty T-shirt."

"Ducks don't eat clothes," grumped Duck.

"And neither should goats. You'll get a stomachache."

"Oh, will I?" grumbled Goat.

Now the great gray cloud was

GINORMOUS!

It was a great gray blob hanging low overhead,

so now ALL the animals were grumpy.

Then something strange began to happen.
The great gray cloud turned blue and purple
and yellow until it was

BLACK!

Sitting beneath this ginormous black cloud were . . .

a dog who	a pig whose	a rooster	a rabbit who
had stopped	ears were	who was	had lost his
wagging his	droopy,	no longer	hop,
tail,		cockadoodling,	

a tortoise who had decided to stay in his shell forever and ever,

a goat who scowled at the big black cloud,

and a duck who was still grumpy.

What sort of cloud was it?

Was it a GLOOM cloud?

Or a MOOD cloud?

Could it be . . . was it . . .

a GRUMPY DUCK cloud?

Would it blot out the sun forever?

Could it BURST?

YES!

Suddenly there were . . .

SPLATT PLOP
PLINK PLITTER PLATT DRIBBLE

MILLIONS OF BIG SHINY

WET SPLASHY RAINDROPS!

Duck spread her wings wide open.

She splished and splashed and sploshed.

Duck wasn't grumpy anymore.

"I'm waddling in the rain.

QUACK! QUACK!"

she sang.

WOOF
WOOF

OINK OINK

BLEAT

One by one, they all joined in.

"I'm plopping in the rain. OINK! OINK!"

"I'm barking in the rain. WOOF! WOOF!"

"I'm COCKADOODLING in the rain!"

"I'm hopping so high. HIP-HOP!"

"I'm drinking up the rain. SLURP! SLURP!"

COCKADOODLE-DO

HIP-HOP

QUACK
QUACK

SLURP SLURP

"What a glorious feeling," bleated Goat.
"We're happy again, just waddling, and paddling,
by the pond," they all sang in chorus.
And where was the big black cloud?

Gone!

In its place

was a bright shining

RAINBOW.

THE END

31192021639438